S0-AHJ-858

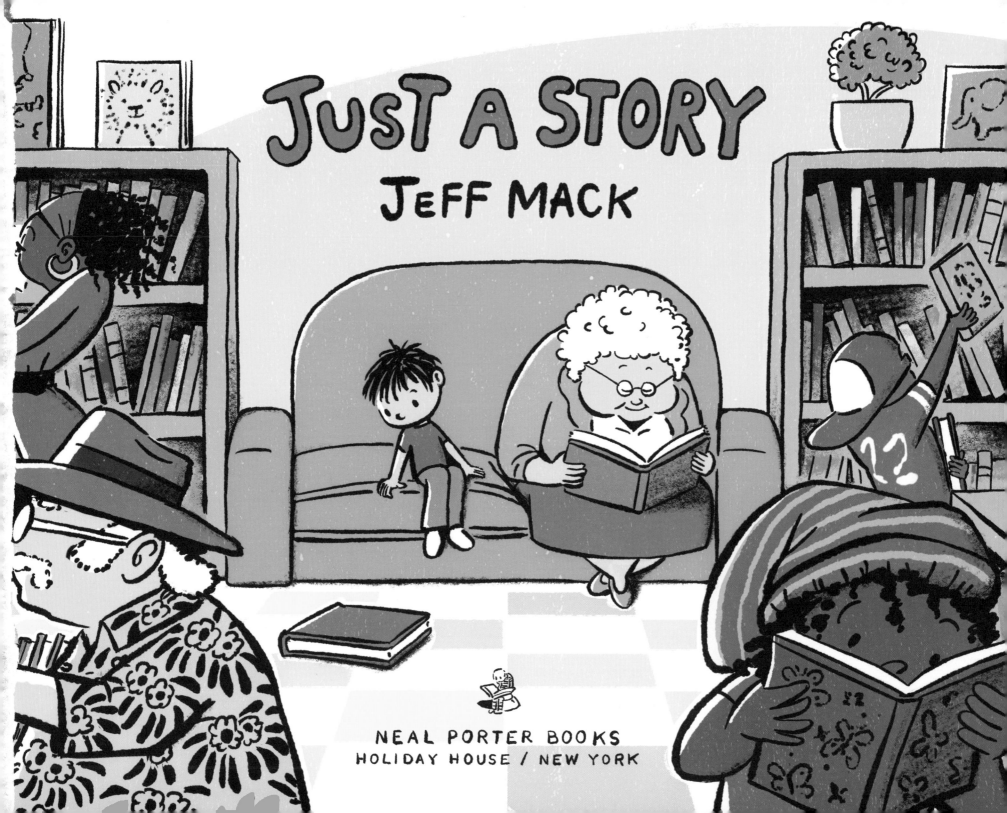

JUST A STORY

JEFF MACK

NEAL PORTER BOOKS
HOLIDAY HOUSE / NEW YORK

For Jenny and the pets

Neal Porter Books

Text and illustrations copyright © 2020 by Jeff Mack
All Rights Reserved
HOLIDAY HOUSE is registered in the U.S. Patent and Trademark Office.
Printed and bound in May 2020 by Toppan Leefung, DongGuan City, China.
The artwork for this book was created with a laptop and a tablet.
Book design by Jennifer Browne
www.holidayhouse.com
First Edition
10 9 8 7 6 5 4 3 2 1

Library of Congress Cataloging-in-Publication Data

Names: Mack, Jeff, author, illustrator.
Title: Just a story / by Jeff Mack.
Description: First edition. | New York : Holiday House, [2020] | Audience:
    Ages 4-8 | Audience: Grades K-1 | Summary: "A young reader comes upon an
    alluring book and he starts to read, becoming blissfully unaware of
    increasingly odd and outlandish occurrences looming all around him"—
    Provided by publisher.
Identifiers: LCCN 2019022729 | ISBN 9780823446636 (hardcover)
Subjects: CYAC: Books and reading—Fiction. | Adventure and
    adventurers—Fiction. | Imagination—Fiction.
Classification: LCC PZ7.M18973 Jus 2020 | DDC [E]—dc23
LC record available at https://lccn.loc.gov/2019022729

This is just a story

about a boy

who was almost
captured by pirates

and then

almost eaten
by a lion

and then almost trampled by a herd of wild elephants

and then almost stomped on

by a big baby dragon

and then
almost squished

by a belly-flopping blue whale

. . . worst of all . . . .

. . . almost . . . .

. . . kissed!

But not quite.

Actually, there was nothing to worry about.

Know why?

Because
this is just a story.